CUNNING CRIMES

More Detective Files to open...

Look out for...

20 CUNNING CRIMES

SHERLOCK RANSFORD
(Det. Insp. Retd.)

Illustrated by
A. Mycroft Merfy
(alias The Red Herring)

Hippo

Scholastic Children's Books,
Commonwealth House, 1–19 New Oxford Street
London WC1A 1NU, UK

A division of Scholastic Ltd
London ~ New York ~ Toronto ~ Sydney ~ Auckland

First published in the UK by Scholastic Ltd, 1986
This edition published by Scholastic Ltd, 1997

Text copyright © Complete Editions Ltd, 1986
Inside illustrations copyright © Complete Editions Ltd, 1986
Cover illustration copyright © Martin Chatterton, 1997

ISBN 0 590 19256 6

All rights reserved
Printed by Cox & Wyman Ltd, Reading, Berks

10 9 8 7 6 5 4 3 2 1

Contents

THE CASE OF THE VALUABLE VALENTINES

IT IS FEBRUARY 13TH AND GOLDFINGERS OF BOND STREET IS SELLING HEART-SHAPED TRINKETS AS VALENTINES.

WEALTHY CUSTOMERS HAVE BEEN GOING IN AND OUT ALL DAY.

AT LUNCH TIME THE SHOP IS PACKED.

7

The Case of the Extraordinary Easter Eggs

Not many people knew that Mr Pearson – Jack to his family and a few close friends – the quiet, balding, middle-aged man who kept the newsagent's and general store in Little Biggington, was a secret agent. His wife, to whom he had been contentedly married for twenty-five years, didn't know, nor did his student daughter, nor his brother, nor his mother, nor any of the 500 inhabitants of Little Biggington.

Life for the Pearsons had run uneventfully and smoothly for many years. Every day, Mr Pearson opened the shop, organized the paper rounds, supplied the villagers with their groceries, and, in the evenings, after taking the dog for its usual constitutional, he would settle down and get on with his latest woodwork project. For he was an enthusiastic carpenter.

The only change in this routine came when

the family took its summer holiday – two weeks by the sea in late July – and on occasional weekends when Mr Pearson went to see his aged mother who lived in a suburb of London. He always went alone, as everyone knew that Mrs Pearson senior did not care for company, and he never said much afterwards about what his mother was doing or what they had talked about, for everyone knew that Mrs Pearson's life was not a very exciting one. If questioned, her son always said he didn't want to bore people with the details.

However, one year, in late February, as the leaves were just coming out on the willows and alders that lined Biggington Brook, Jack Pearson's wife realized that over the past few weeks there had been a change in her husband. He seemed, on the one hand, to be more absent-minded than usual, and on the other, to have become very fussy about his possessions, always checking with his wife if she had moved this or that in his little workroom, and asking her to let him know which days she dusted in there.

He also started to eat eggs for breakfast, or at any rate, the yolks of eggs. He always refused to eat the whites. This change of routine may not sound very important or exciting, but for someone as regular in his habits as Jack Pearson it was very strange indeeed. For as long as Mrs Pearson could remember, her husband's breakfast had consisted of two slices of toast and marmalade and a cup of strong tea. But one day, he had returned from his walk with the dog carrying a dozen new-laid eggs from the farm up the road, and asked if he could have one hard-boiled every morning for breakfast. Mrs Pearson asked what was wrong with the eggs they sold in the store, but her husband insisted that, as the farm eggs were free range and very fresh, they were better than anything they sold. So she did as he asked.

He was also very strange about the order in which the eggs were taken out of the rack for boiling, and would line them up himself and insist that they were only taken out and eaten from left to right. Mrs Pearson protested sometimes, but when he said he was preparing some special eggs for an Easter treat she agreed to use the eggs as he had suggested.

But apart from this unusual fussiness about his room, and his odd behaviour about the eggs, nothing seemed changed in Jack Pearson's life. The family routine continued as usual, and Easter drew near. On the Monday before the holiday weekend, Jack set out at six o'clock as usual with the dog. Half an hour later the animal returned panting, with a note fixed to its collar, which read: "Hard boil the eggs in the rack and open them on Easter Day".

Mrs Pearson was extremely puzzled. Nothing so strange had ever happened in her life before, and she began to think that Jack was perhaps going a little mad. But then, thinking that this was part of his Easter-egg surprise,

Mrs Pearson decided to wait until her husband returned. When it got to 7.30 pm, though, she began to get a little worried. When he still hadn't returned at 9 pm, she rang the police.

The police thought she was a silly woman and said Mr Pearson had likely gone off to the pub with a friend. Mrs Pearson protested that he had never done such a thing in twenty-five years of married life, but the policeman said there was always a first time and rang off.

But the next morning, when Mr Pearson still had not returned, the police began to take the matter more seriously and agreed to look for him. But, though they searched the whole area, they found nothing whatsoever to indicate what had happened to him. Jack Pearson seemed to have vanished into thin air.

Meanwhile, his poor wife was in a terrible state. She didn't know what to do or what to think. Then she remembered the strange message on the dog's collar – the message she had dismissed as an Easter prank. There were two eggs left in the rack. She looked at each one carefully but could see nothing unusual about them. So, having great faith in her husband and not too much imagination, she decided to follow his instructions exactly. On Easter Day, she boiled the two eggs together in a pan for ten minutes, let them go cold, and then began to peel off the shells. As she did so she was astonished to find a number of strange marks on the white of each egg. This is what they looked like:

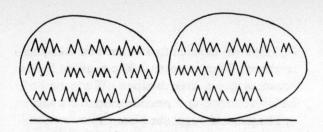

Mrs Pearson studied the marks carefully for some time. After a while it occurred to her that they reminded her of something. When she was young, Mrs Pearson had beeen a Girl Guide, and one of the things she had been especially good at was transcribing Morse code. That was what the marks on the eggs reminded her of – the long and short taps, or dashes and dots, of the code. She rushed into the living-room and hunted through the bookshelves for her old Guide handbook. At last – there it was. She turned to the page that gave the code. This is what it looked like:

A	.-	M	--	Y	-.--
B	-...	N	-.	Z	--..
C	-.-.	O	---	1	.----
D	-..	P	.--.	2	..---
E	.	Q	--.-	3	...--
F	..-.	R	.-.	4	....-
G	--.	S	...	5	.....
H	....	T	-	6	-....
I	..	U	..-	7	--...
J	.---	V	...-	8	---..
K	-.-	W	.--	9	----.
L	.-..	X	-..-	0	-----

But Mrs Pearson knew that you could also transcribe it as shown on the eggs, so she sat down with a piece of paper and a pencil and produced a copy of the code written out in high and low peaks. It looked like this:

A H O V

B I P W

C J Q X

D K R Y

E L S Z

F M T

G N U

1 6

2 7

3 8

4 9

5 10

Using it, can you read the message on the eggs and find out what happened to Mr Pearson?

A Likely Winner

On an April morning of bright sunshine and scudding white clouds driven by a fresh south-westerly wind, a string of racehorses were making their way to the Downland Gallops. They gleamed in the sun, snatched at their bits, and danced sideways as the wind whipped up the corners of their exercise blankets. Trainer Bill Andrews followed them in his Land Rover, casting a critical eye over each horse. They were being prepared for the classic races of the flat-racing season which had just started, and he had high hopes for several of them, especially Set Fair, and her jockey, Ben Bridges.

That morning Set Fair went very well, and her lad gave her a good report. "If she keeps going like this, Mr Andrews, she'll be a dead cert for the Newmarket Cup next month!"

"That's what I want to hear," grinned Bill. "Bridges'll be here next week – we'll see what he thinks. She goes better for him than for anybody."

On the other side of the Downs, Charlie Taylor was preparing his horses for the season, too. His great hope for the Newmarket Cup was a big brown colt called Night Must Fall, which was to be ridden by Dave Duncan.

"You'll have a very good chance," he told Dave. "Your only rival will be Ben Bridges on Set Fair. They seem to be an unbeatable combination."

"We'll see about that," growled Dave.

But as the day of the big race drew nearer, it seemed as if the public agreed with Charlie Taylor. Nearly all the bets were on Set Fair, and Terry Griggs, the local bookie, was in despair. "I'll be ruined if Set Fair wins," he grumbled. "What shall I do then?"

Bill Andrews was boxing Set Fair, and his other Newmarket Cup day runners, over to East Anglia on the day before the race. Never had Set Fair looked fitter. Her chestnut coat rippled over her firm muscles, and Bill had no doubt he was sending a winner to Newmarket.

Ben Bridges was riding at Newbury that day, so he decided to drive himself over to Newmarket on the morning of the race. He was keen on cars as well as horses, and his silver-grey Mercedes sports car was well known around the Downs.

On the morning before the big day things were not going well at Charlie Taylor's yard. He, too, was sending his Newmarket runners that day, but the horsebox had broken down. Charlie knew nothing of the workings of cars – he had never even looked under the bonnet of his own – and was cursing and fuming, because the local garage could not promise to send out a mechanic until after lunch. Freddie, the head lad, went to see what the matter was.

"Can you fix this thing?" Charlie roared. "I hate motors. They always let you down. Give me horses any day!"

Freddie had a look at it but shook his head. "It's beyond me, guv. But isn't Dave Duncan around? He knows all there is to know about engines. I'm sure he'll fix it for you."

Sure enough, when Dave arrived on the scene he fixed the horsebox, and it set out just before lunch, taking Night Must Fall, two lads and two other horses to Newmarket.

Meanwhile, Ben Bridges was having a good day at the Newbury races. He won twice and came second on his third ride of the day. He was the hero of the hour, and the excitement built up at the thought of the next day's big race. Bill Andrews went to put on his bet and met a long-faced Terry Griggs.

"Cor blimey Mr Andrews – if you and

Bridges go on like this I'll be ruined! I've a good mind not to go tomorrow, but my wife's sister lives at Newmarket and I've promised we'll go to see her. It's her birthday tomorrow, you see."

Bill sympathised. He knew what Terry's wife was like. She chauffeured Terry everywhere, as he had never learnt to drive and disliked cars. Because of this he seemed to be under her power.

"Sorry, Terry," said Bill. "But – though I don't want to ruin you – I hope we do win tomorrow. I've never had a Newmarket Cup winner so it's all very exciting for me. Anyway, you bookies never go broke!"

Ben Bridges wisely took no notice of the celebrations going on around him, but went home to get a good night's sleep.

His alarm clock roused him at seven. The sky was overcast and he wondered if it would rain later. He got his breakfast, filled a flask with coffee for the journey, packed an overnight bag – for he was going to stay at Newmarket that night – and went out to put his belongings in the Mercedes, which he kept parked in the road outside his house. By eight o'clock he was bowling along through the countryside, whistling cheerfully as he contemplated the day ahead.

Set Fair had settled down after her journey and was all ready for the race. Bill Andrews strode up and down outside her stable, glancing anxiously at his watch. "It's nearly one o'clock. Ben should be here by now," he muttered. "I expected him by twelve at the latest. Surely he can't have overslept, today of all days."

A racehorse official hurried up to him, interrupting his thoughts. "Mr Andrews, there's terrible news. Ben Bridges' car crashed near Cambridge. Seems it went out of control down a hill. He's been taken to hospital with multiple injuries."

It subsequently transpired that, apart from a number of cuts and bruises, the only major injury Ben had suffered was a broken leg. But, of course, there was no riding of Set Fair in the Newmarket Cup and Night Must Fall won by a length. Charlie Taylor was thrilled, Dave Duncan delighted, and poor Terry Griggs was so overcome he even enjoyed his sister-in-law's birthday party. But Bill Andrews was puzzled. Ben was a good and careful driver, unlikely to take foolish risks. He kept his car in tip-top condition, too. And Bill had heard no other vehicle was involved. It all seemed very odd.

Bill wasn't the only person to think so. The next day he received a visit from the police who were investigating the cause of the accident.

"I'm afraid we have some rather unpleasant news, sir," said the young policeman who called. "It seems to be a case of attempted murder. The near-side front brake pipe was severed. It seems to have been very cleverly cut through so as to snap at a particular moment. Do you know of anyone who might have wanted to do this to Ben Bridges?"

Who cut through Ben Bridges' brake pipe?

THE CASE OF THE DRIFFIELD DIAMOND

LORD AND LADY DRIFFIELD HAVE OPENED MIDDLETON MANOR TO THE PUBLIC.

ONE OF THE MOST POPULAR SIGHTS WITH VISITORS IS THE FAMOUS DRIFFIELD DIAMOND, SAID TO BRING BAD LUCK TO ALL WHO POSSESS IT.

IT IS GUARDED NIGHT AND DAY. ONE MORNING, JUST AFTER OPENING TIME, THE ALARM GOES OFF IN THE NEXT ROOM...

DRRIINNG!

The Fanshawe Family Mystery

"They say young Rupert Fanshawe's turned up."

"Rupert Fanshawe? Who's he? Never heard of him."

"Octavia's son. Remember that scandal thirty years ago when she went off to Canada? They say she had a son out there – that's who Rupert Fanshawe is."

"Well, there's a turn-up for the book. I wonder what the old lady thinks about it?"

The regulars at the *Horse and Furrow* had a new topic of conversation that evening. The Fanshawes were an ancient family, who had lived at Ashover Hall since one of their ancestors had been awarded the manor by a grateful Edward III, for valour at the Battle of Crécy in 1346. The house and land had always passed to a male descendant, but old Colonel Fanshawe, the previous owner, had had no son, just two daughters, Augusta and Octavia. The former's fiancé had been killed when he was a young man, and Augusta had never married. Octavia, the daughter the customers at the *Horse and Furrow* had referred to, had indeed left the country after rumour of a scandal. And so, when Miss Augusta died, the entire house and its contents and land were to be left to the National Trust. Augusta felt that future generations would like to see a family home that had remained virtually untouched for six centuries, and, though she was sad she had no children to bequeath the Hall to, she felt she was doing the right thing in leaving it to the Trust. If Octavia had had a son, things might have been different. . .

The morning after the conversation had taken place in the *Horse and Furrow*, there was a ring at the bell at the Hall's front door. Mrs Andrews, the daily help, answered it, for the family fortunes didn't run to butlers these days, and announced to Miss Augusta that Mr Rupert had arrived from Canada to see his aunt. Accompanying her was a tall, dark-haired, blue-eyed young man, who bore a resemblance to the portrait of Colonel Fanshawe as a young man which hung in the hall. He wore a well-cut business suit and had a gold signet ring on the third finger of his right hand. Self-confident and quite at his ease, he addressed Augusta Fanshawe as follows.

"Hello, Aunt Augusta. I'm Rupert – Octavia's son. I'm sorry if this is a bit of a shock but I thought it was time to come and see the family home. I'm thinking of getting married, to an English girl, and we like the thought of living here. Of course, we'd keep a flat in London. . ."

Poor Augusta Fanshawe was nonplussed. She had never even been sure that she had a nephew – but for him to turn up on the doorstep claiming her house as his – it was just too much! Octavia had never answered her letters all those years before, and as time passed she had assumed that either her sister was dead, or that she didn't want to have any connection with the family. Either way, Ashover Hall had been her home for sixty years and she was not going to surrender it lightly.

"I think you assume too much, young man," she replied coldly. "I was not even aware that Octavia had a son. She never told me of your existence."

Rupert's manner was light and relaxed. "Well, you can see that she did. I'm sorry to appear suddenly like this, but it seems to me that Ashover Hall is really mine. I'm the male heir, you see. Of course, as my wife and I shouldn't live here all the time, we'd let you stay on. You could have the apartment in the east wing that old Colonel Fanshawe created for his mother."

He seemed to have some knowledge of the

house, thought Augusta, but he was not going to gain control of it that easily. They parted with mutual mutterings about contacting solicitors.

Two days later Augusta had another caller. Mrs Andrews announced, "There's young Mr Fanshawe again, ma'am," and ushered in the young man who had called the day before. This time he wore a tweed suit with, incongruously, a black tie, and looked altogether more suitably dressed for the country than he had done on his previous visit.

"What do you want this time?" asked Augusta coldly. The young man looked puzzled.

"I'm so sorry to arrive without telephoning first. I tried last night but couldn't get through. Perhaps you didn't get my letter? I'm Rupert Fanshawe, your sister Octavia's son. I've lived in Canada until now, but my mother died last month and I got a longing to see the old family home, and to meet you. Mother wouldn't let me come when she was still alive. I do hope you don't mind me calling."

Augusta looked bewildered. "But you were here two days ago," she blurted out. "You said you wanted to marry an English girl and live in my house – in Ashover Hall."

At this the young man looked bewildered. "Two days ago I was in Montreal," he said. "I flew over yesterday, stayed in London last night and got the train down here this morning. I've never been here before. I recognized the Hall from photographs."

Augusta studied him keenly. Her eyesight was not as good as it had been, and when she looked at the young man more closely she thought that maybe he was not the same person who had called before. He had the same dark, curly hair, the same blue eyes, but he was perhaps not as tall as the first Rupert. His manner was different, too. This Rupert seemed rather shy and unsure of himself, though his eyes were friendly. Augusta noticed he wore no gold ring.

That afternoon, after she had persuaded the young man to go and stay in a hotel until the puzzle was sorted out, she went to see Mr Pendlebury of Oldsworth and Pendlebury, solicitors to the Fanshawes for 120 years. She told him as much as she could about the bewildering visits of the two Ruperts and asked him what she should do. Mr Pendlebury was sad to see his client so upset. He tried to reassure her by pointing out that the young men couldn't both be Rupert Fanshawe – if indeed either of them were – and that he had better start making enquiries.

"I'll contact the Canadian authorities first, to see if there is any record of a son being born to Octavia. And if there is, I'll try and find out more about him. I don't want to worry you, my dear, but this is a very strange business, and a lot of money could be at stake. Be very careful

what you do for the next few days, and don't
hesitate to contact me if you are worried."

Mr Pendlebury hired two private detectives
to keep an eye on the two Ruperts while he
pursued several lines of enquiry in Canada. A
few days later, Augusta received a letter.

Westgate Chambers
Middlehampton
Tuesday

My Dear Miss Augusta,

*I do hope you have a good Easter
Holiday. It is important to have a good
rest, you know. All the medical evidence
points to it!*

*But first, how are you getting on
with young Rupert? I know it is not
an easy task, my dear, to have to
welcome into your family an unknown
nephew, but we all have to take the rough
with the smooth, and I think this is one
of those times.*

I will write another letter to you from Scotland, where I am going for a few days to see Colonel Mackintosh's new livery yard at Stirling.

Once again, my dear, have a good holiday.

With my very best wishes,

Yours,

Howard Pendlebury

P.S. In times of trouble and perplexity, remember the family motto!

The letter had a crumpled appearance, as if it had been through a typewriter more than once, though of course it was hand-written. It even appeared to have a few holes in it. Augusta looked at it for a few moments, frowning as she tried to remember the family motto. What exactly did it say? It was carved over the doorway of the former great hall, where dances and banquets had been held in the old days, and which was hardly used at all now. She squinted up at it, trying to read the message in the gloom: "Let the light shine forth among darkness." What a strange thing for Mr Pendlebury to put on his letter!

She went out into the daylight and held up the letter. Suddenly she smiled, and rushed upstairs to pack her bag, for she had a train to catch.

What was the message she received?

A Shot In The Dark

The Country House Murder, a play by a well-known thriller writer, had been running in London's West End for a year, with a virtually unchanged cast. Heading it was the *grande dame* of the stage, Lily Lajeune, who played Marguerite Massingham, widow of Colonel Massingham, who lived in The Mulberries, a large and beautiful house in Berkshire, with a garden stretching down to the Thames. The play was set in the late 1940s, and Marguerite Massingham was a classic character – rich, elegant, a leading light at the Women's Institute, an upright but kindly woman.

Lily Lajeune was not much like the character she played. She had been on the stage for thirty years, and from the time she had played her first roles she had maintained a very superior attitude towards her colleagues. But she was a good actress, and soon began to take leading roles. This made her even more impossible, and very unpopular with her fellow actors and actresses. She told them all what to do, bullied the juniors, was sarcastic to the other actresses, and refused to work with leading men of whom she did not approve.

Her leading man in *The Country House Murder* was Henry Proctor, who played Detective Inspector David Williams, the sharp-brained policeman who solves the case. He, also, had been in the profession for many years, but was just the opposite of Lily, being good-humoured and friendly towards everyone. Maybe that was why he agreed to work with her. However, by the end of the year his patience was wearing thin and he felt he could not take much more of Lily. He hoped to leave the cast as soon as he had found another good part. Good parts seemed to be few and far between, though, which was why he was still playing the part of Detective Inspector Williams.

Lily's sister was also in the play. Her stage name was Jennifer Latham – in fact it was her real name, but Lily had felt that Latham sounded dull so she had called herself Lajeune. Jennifer played a friend of Marguerite's who was staying at The Mulberries, called Sally Porter. Jennifer was five years younger than Lily, though the latter maintained that *she* looked *years* younger. And she was a very different kind of woman. She had always had to live in the shadow of her sister's success, and was always given the less important parts. She had learned to accept this and didn't mind it too much – but what she hated was the way her sister treated her in front of the other members of the cast. Away from the theatre the two sisters seldom saw each other, but when they were working together Lily was always unpleasant to Jennifer. She would refer to her as "the stupid daughter of the family" or "the plain one" – or sometimes even try and pretend that Jennifer was not her sister. So Jennifer was getting extremely tired of Lily, and she too was trying to leave the cast, vowing that this was the last time she would take part in the same play as her sister.

Everyone was surprised that Lily herself was still there, for she usually got bored with long runs. But she did not show any signs of leaving this one, much to the disgust of her understudy, Selma Price. Selma had a part in the play, that of Mrs Nelson the housekeeper, but it was not a very big part and she longed for the chance to play Marguerite Massingham. She had done so for only two nights in the run, when Lily had had laryngitis, which, sadly for Selma, cleared up very quickly. So Selma bided her time and waited for Lily to get fed up and leave, telling the rest of the cast that she suspected that no one else wanted Lily as her reputation had become so bad.

But of course the audiences didn't know that.

Lily Lajeune was as popular as ever with them and had lots of fans. Each night the play had been on, the house had been packed – which kept the theatre management happy. So they didn't listen to any complaints about Lily, and everyone had to put up with her.

The murder in the play took place in the second act. Marguerite was shot by an unknown person through the French windows. The scene was a summer night and the windows were open on to the dark garden to let in the cool night air. Marguerite had to cross the drawing-room, which was the main set of the play, to go to the kitchen to check that she had left Mrs Nelson's instructions for the morning on the table. At this time "Mrs Nelson" – that is, Selma Price – was supposed to have already gone up to bed, but in reality she was in her dressing-room changing into her nightdress and dressing-gown and having curlers put in her hair so she could rush downstairs and discover the body at the appropriate moment. Henry Proctor, who didn't appear in the play until the second act, was also in his dressing-room at this time, having the finishing touches put to his make-up.

On the night of the 325th performance the atmosphere backstage was even worse than usual. There had been a big row that afternoon when the producer, Brian Marshall, had suggested, very gently, that maybe the scene in which Marguerite first met her second cousin

who had come to stay and who was eventually denounced as the murderer, could be played slightly differently. Lily had stormed up and down saying that the way she played it had satisfied everyone up to now and that she had no intention of changing it. Most members of the cast agreed with the producer, but in the end he, and they, had to give in and Lily got her own way as usual.

So the curtain rose on the 325th performance, and when Lily appeared on the stage the audience clapped enthusiastically. She played the scene with the cousin as she had always played it, and by the tumultuous applause at the end of the first act, congratulated herself that she had been right after all. She had always known that she was, of course.

The second act began. It was set in the evening, after a late dinner, and the party was drinking coffee in the drawing-room. One by one they excused themselves and went up to bed, Sally Porter being the first to leave. Marguerite put the cups on a tray ready for Mrs Nelson in the morning, and began to walk across the room towards the kitchen. Right on cue a shot rang out, and Lily crumpled to the ground, as she had done 324 times before. Only this time a thin stream of blood trickled from her still form to make an ever-increasing pool on the carpet covering the stage. . .

The curtain fell as it always did, but this time the audience heard a scream from behind it, and a lot of rushing about. The curtain did not rise again. Instead, the theatre manager, white-faced and shaking, appeared in front of the curtain.

"Ladies and gentlemen," he began. "I am sorry to inform you that there has been an accident, and I'm afraid the play cannot continue tonight. Please proceed in an orderly fashion to the box office, where your ticket money will be refunded."

The audience was greatly shocked, but it was not until they saw the newspapers the next morning that the real tragedy struck them. Lily Lajeune was dead. A real shot had been fired through the French windows.

Who killed her?

THE CASE OF THE MISSING MANUSCRIPT

THIS IS MILLBROOK MUSEUM, WHICH HOUSES MANY MEDIEVAL TREASURES...

...INCLUDING A PRICELESS ILLUMINATED MANUSCRIPT IN ROOM 42.

BILL AND ALF, THE SECURITY GUARDS, CHECK THAT ALL IS WELL AT 4.50 P.M.

BUT WHEN THEY RETURN TO LOCK UP AT 5 P.M. . . . .

. . . THE CASE IS OPEN AND THE MANUSCRIPT HAS VANISHED!

ONLY FOUR PEOPLE HAVE VISITED ROOM 42 IN THOSE TEN MINUTES AND THE GUARDS SAW THEM LEAVE.

WHICH OF THE FOUR IS THE ONLY ONE WHO COULD HAVE STOLEN THE MANUSCRIPT?

Shopping For Gold

F. M. Harrison & Co. had a discreet frontage in London's Hatton Garden. But, in the street that ran behind it, was the entrance to a garage large enough to contain several delivery vans. For Harrisons were shippers of gold bullion.

The company had been in business for over a hundred years with only one attempted theft – in 1885 – until the last two years. Since then there had been four successful robberies, in which the company had lost nearly three million pounds, and two unsuccessful ones, in which the gold had been recovered, though the criminals were never caught. So worried were Harrisons that in desperation they had hit upon a new security device. Their armoured delivery vans were used as decoys, following a different route from those which carried the precious cargo, and the bullion was transported in tradesmen's vans. "C. R. Jones, Fresh Fish,"

"Dan Hamilton, Fresh Fruit and Veg Daily," and "Watson & Co., Plumbing and Heating Experts," were some of those used.

Yet one of the four robberies had taken place since these elaborate precautions had been set up. Harrisons were at their wits' end and didn't know what to do.

"Let's give it one more go this Friday with the fish van," said John Bryant, the transport manager. "They got the plumbers, but they can't possibly know about this one."

And so it was arranged. At 3 pm on Friday, 13th May, "C. R. Jones, Fresh Fish," was to carry two million pounds' worth of gold bullion from the vaults in Hatton Garden to Heathrow Airport. The operation was veiled in secrecy.

Everything seemed to go according to plan. Yet, at precisely seven minutes past three, C. R. Jones's van was held up in High Holborn and its cargo stolen. Harrisons were mystified as to how the criminals could have known the gold was in the fishmonger's van. Scotland Yard were mystified, too, when they arrived. "It must be someone in the company passing on information," they said.

Mr Williams, the Managing Director, rubbed his forehead. "But how could that be? All our staff are completely trustworthy and have worked here for years."

"Is there anyone new?" asked Inspector Kirk, the man in charge of the Yard operation.

"No, I don't think so."

"Anyone temporary, or part-time?"

"No – oh, wait a minute, we do sometimes employ a temporary typist from the agency. They don't always send the same girl, though."

"May I see where she works?" asked the Inspector.

He searched the small office, the desk, the cupboard, and was about to give up when the wastepaper bin caught his eye. He fished out a crumpled piece of paper. It was the carbon copy of a very long and complicated shopping list. "Odd to type out your shopping list *and* make a copy," thought the Inspector.

He looked at it again. The prices seemed wildly optimistic these days, he thought, reading it more carefully. In fact they were absurd, probably not prices at all...

Suddenly his brow cleared. "Which agency do you use for your typists, Mr Williams?" he asked. "I think we've found your mole."

Here is the shopping list. *Can you see how the thieves received their tip-off?*

fish fingers	1p/5p
ice-cream	1p
carrots	7p
yoghurt	4p
vanilla essence	1p
bread	4p
lentils	3p

garlic	4p
tomatoes	7p
beans	3p
vinegar	1p
macaroni	9p
pineapple	3p
aubergines	6p
3 pears	1p
turnip	6p
pumpkin	3p
Roquefort	6p
capers	5p
milk	2p
potted meat	6p
yams	2p
pastry	6p
vine leaves	1p
wine	2p
watercress	2p
honey	1p
apple pie	7p
ginger	1p/3p
Cheddar	2p
herbs	1p
cornflakes	2p
walnuts	3p
gooseberries	6p
flour	3p
sugar	5p
onions	2p/5p

Take A Bow

It was a sunny day in early June and Fenton Oliver had just won the Under Eighteens Archery Championship. A family celebration was planned at his grandfather's house – of all the Olivers, old Mr Christopher had the best facilities for entertaining.

So Fenton set out that Saturday morning with his young brother James, his teenage sister Isobel, and their mother, Maria, who, in her childhood, had also been a keen archer. His older brother, Edward, who worked for the government in London, was to make his own way down to Five Oaks, his grandfather's house in Hampshire.

Fenton's father was dead. He had been killed six years before, when Fenton was eleven, in a car crash. He had always been a reckless man and it was thought that he had probably been driving a great deal too fast when a steering fault on his Jaguar caused him to go off the road and into a tree. He had been killed instantly.

However, no such thoughts were passing through the heads the Olivers as they motored over to Five Oaks in the June sunshine. They enjoyed visits to grandfather, for though he was rather eccentric he managed to make family gatherings fun, and his housekeeper, Mrs Bell, was a splendid cook.

It was 11.30 when the car turned in the gateway of Five Oaks. Grandfather Oliver must have heard it, for he came down the steps to greet them as they drew up at the front door.

"Welcome, welcome, my dears." He kissed them each in turn. "And congratulations, young Fenton. Have you brought your bow and arrows? I'm expecting a demonstration of your skills after lunch. Look – there on the lawn – there's a target I've put up specially."

"Don't worry, Grandpa," said Fenton. "I've even brought a spare bow."

The lawn at Five Oaks was in front of the house, screened by a high wall and the trees of its name from the road and the drive. There, in its centre, was a professional-looking archery target specially purchased for the occasion by Mr Oliver.

"Good-oh," exclaimed James excitedly. "Can I have a go? Fenton won't let me at home."

"I should think not," said his mother firmly. "If you started shooting arrows around on *our*

lawn there's no knowing what might happen. There's not as much space in Reading as there is here."

She and Fenton and Isobel went into the house, glad of the chance to escape from the hot sunshine for a while. But James went tearing about in his usual demented manner, examining everything he could find to make sure nothing had changed since his last visit. He loved Five Oaks.

Mrs Bell had prepared a cold lunch which they decided to eat in a shady corner of the garden. They had just finished setting out the cutlery, glasses, crockery and chairs when the sound of an engine running announced the arrival of Edward. He looked hot and rather cross.

"Sorry I'm late, grandfather," he grimaced. "The traffic out of London was terrible – the car was overheating and I had to pull off the road for a while to let it cool down." It seemed as if Edward, for all his dull-sounding civil service job, was the one most likely to take after his father. Already, at twenty-two, he had owned a number of fast and disreputable cars which frequently broke down, due, his mother suspected, to his habit of fixing their engines with devices to make them go faster which were designed for altogether racier models. But she didn't interfere, for she knew that trying to persuade her eldest son to behave differently had the effect of making him stick ever more obstinately to his chosen course of action.

At lunch, after the archery competition had been discussed in detail, and the young champion toasted in champagne, the talk turned to money.

"I hope you are managing all right, my dear." Grandfather was addressing Mrs Oliver, who, since becoming a widow, had returned to work full-time at the local hospital, where she was a laboratory technician.

"Oh, yes, fine," she replied. She was a proud woman who had always refused offers of financial help, telling Grandfather to save his money for her children. He was fond of telling them that he was an old man and that, on his death – which might not be far away – his money would go to them.

Maria Oliver was much more concerned about her children's financial position than about her own. Edward, it was true, had a job, but he was constantly in debt owing to his hobby of playing around with fast cars. She couldn't see how Fenton's archery skills could be of much use when it came to earning a living, and she had to admit that he didn't show any other talents at present. Isobel was a dreamer, full of fantastic ideas of training to be a dancer, or going on the stage, or of becoming a fashion designer. Yet she seemed reluctant to take any practical step towards the realization of these dreams. And as for young James ... She smiled to herself. He would probably be the biggest success of them all on the job front, she thought, if his energy and enthusiasm lasted into adulthood.

In fact, each of the Oliver children felt in need of a good deal of money – and the sooner the better. In James's case this was to replace the miniature motorbike his friend Michael had lent him before going off to the East. But Michael would be back at school in September, and new bikes of that sort cost a good deal of money. James didn't know what to do.

Isobel needed money to pay the fees of the dancing school at which she had secretly enrolled; Fenton desperately wanted to go on a young sportsmen's tour and series of demonstrations in the States; and Edward had run up greater debts than anyone dreamed of on his cars. Each one of them was desperate, and each one of them had kept it a secret from the rest of the family and from their friends.

Still, on this glorious day after a delicious lunch such thoughts seemed far away. After the dishes had been taken in and washed up, Grandfather Oliver insisted on Fenton giving his archery demonstration, and the family gathered on the lawn.

One by one Fenton's arrows thudded into the target, each a perfect shot. "Bravo!" called out Grandfather. Isobel, who didn't care for sports of any kind, looked bored, and wandered off in search of a book to while away the long, hot afternoon. Edward, who was always irritated by his young brother's skill, muttered something about checking his radiator, and disappeared in the direction of the garage. James was leaping up and down asking when he could have his go.

"Hold your horses," laughed Fenton. "I've got to get these out of the target first."

Grandfather helped him release the arrows, then Fenton returned to where James was waiting eagerly. He showed him how to hold the bow, how to stretch it forwards against the string, how to hold the arrow so its flight did not interfere with the action of the bow. James was itching to release the arrow. Fenton was just telling him that he would have to wait until Grandfather had moved well away from the target when there was a whistling sound from the trees behind them. An arrow shot through the air and Grandfather fell to the ground.

Who killed Grandfather Oliver?

THE CASE OF THE SINISTER SAFE

THE SMYTHSON-SMYTHES OF LAMERTON LODGE KEEP THEIR VALUABLES IN A SAFE THAT CAN ONLY BE OPENED BY A LEFT-HANDED PERSON.

LAMERTON LODGE IS BEING REPAIRED AND REDECORATED — THERE ARE MEN MENDING THE ROOF...

...PAINTING THE WINDOW FRAMES...

The Greek Island Kidnap

The Llewellyns' summer holiday was not a good one that year for Anthony. His father was a diplomat, and most years they would go away for a month, renting a house in some exotic part of the world. Anthony would take his friend Bill. They were both only children, so both sets of parents were happy for the boys to have someone to share the holiday with, and the two always had a great time together. But this year, just two days before the flight to Corfu, Bill developed measles and had to stay behind. So Anthony went off with his parents, taking plenty of books – mostly adventure and mystery stories – so he wouldn't be bored on his own. And then, when they had been in Corfu a week, Anthony developed measles too and had to stay in bed. He couldn't even read, for the measles made his eyes sore and he had to stay in a darkened room. What a way to spend a holiday, thought Anthony, stuck in this dark, stuffy room with the sun streaming down outside and the sparkling blue sea to swim in. He couldn't believe his bad luck.

After his son had got over the worst, Mr Llewellyn amused him by writing letters in code. He showed Anthony how to use a code grille, a device consisting of a piece of paper with boxes cut out of it, which was fitted over an innocent-looking letter or other document to reveal a not-so-innocent message;

Dear Christopher,

I thought I would let you know how I'm getting on here in the big City. From Monday to Friday I commute all the way from the suburb of Potter's Bar - when the train arrives it is at least an hour later! I went out to the airport to see Concorde land — tell William John sends his love.

Lots of love,
Brian.

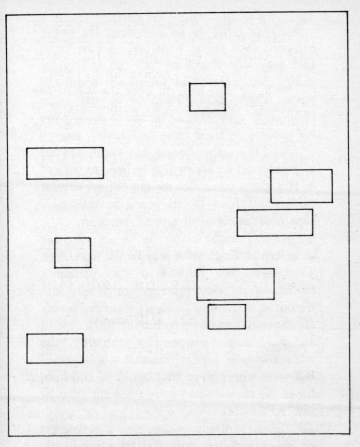

Anthony enjoyed this game very much, and bombarded his father with messages like the one below, using the code grille. Mr Llewellyn was very relieved when his son was allowed out and about again, as he did not find the message-sending quite as exciting as Anthony did. But by this time there were only eight days of the holiday left.

Anthony made up for lost time. He swam, explored rock pools, went out on boat trips, and generally found out all the interesting things that were to be found out about the place. There didn't seem to be any other children to play with, so he had to accompany his parents on their visits to Kérkira, though he found this rather boring. He wasn't allowed to wander off on his own, as he liked to do, and he thought it was much too hot to have to wear clothes and shoes. On the beach he could have kept cool and walked around barefoot.

On the Tuesday before the family were due to return to England it was hotter than ever. They went into Kérkira so that Anthony's mother could buy presents for family and friends at home, and Anthony was very bored. He cheered himself up by buying Bill a copy of an old map, supposedly showing the whereabouts of pirates' treasure – and wished Bill were with him so they could go and hunt for it. As they walked away from the shop he saw an ice-cream vendor.

"Please, Mummy, *please*, may I go and get an ice-cream? It's only just back there, it'll only take a minute." His mother relented, gave him a handful of drachmas, and off he ran.

A few minutes later Mrs Llewellyn turned round from the shop window she had been studying, puzzled that Anthony had not yet returned. He seemed to have been a long time, for as far as she could recall there had been no queue at the ice-cream van. She looked in the direction where it was parked, but the van had gone. Where was Anthony? She walked back down the street, calling him and looking for him in the shops, but there was no sign of him.

She spent perhaps half an hour looking before she began to get worried. Anthony knew he was not allowed to go off on his own in the town, and he was usually an obedient child. What could have happened to him? It was a quarter to twelve. At twelve she was to meet her husband so they could wander around and choose a restaurant for lunch, so she spent the fifteen minutes up until then pacing the street, checking every shop again, and looking out for the ice-cream vendor. But it was no use. There was no sign of either the ice-cream man nor of Anthony. Nor was there any clue as to where he might have gone. He seemed to have vanished into thin air.

The next day the Llewellyns received a typed letter. There was no postmark, so it must have been pushed through the letterbox before the household was stirring. It said: *"We have your son. We want a million pounds – or you will never see him alive again. Do not go to the police. Leave the money in a bag on the second bench on the left at Kérkira bus station on Wednesday evening at 9."*

"Wednesday, that's today," thought Mr Llewellyn. He was a rich man, but not that rich. Not rich enough to be able to find a million pounds in a few hours. He'd gone to the police the afternoon before, after checking all the places his wife had checked. The police had told him that there should have been no ice-cream vendor in that part of town as they were not licensed to operate there. Mrs Llewellyn had not seen the ice-cream man clearly, and was little use as a witness. All she could verify was the time at which her son had disappeared.

Despite the warning on the letter, Mr Llewellyn rang the police, and the British Embassy in Athens. Both suggested that he play for time by leaving a note at the appointed place, saying it would take him a few days to raise the money, and that meanwhile he wanted proof that his son was still alive. And so he followed their advice, looking carefully around the bus station, but seeing no one who looked suspicious – nor any sign of the police.

On Thursday morning there was another message from the kidnappers – and a letter from Anthony. The message said: *"Here is a letter from your son. He is alive and well but will not be unless we get the money. You have until Friday evening at 9. Same place."*

Anthony's letter read as follows:

Dear Mum and Dad.

I am writing to let you know
I am safe and in good health.

Apart from a smell of
ammonia, my room is
OK and I get three square
meals a day though the third is only
cheese on bread.

Don't worry, I'm all right,
and I hope I can come home
soon.

your loving Son,

Anthony

"How very odd that he should write about smells at a time like this," thought Mr Llewellyn. "Ammonia..." He suddenly rushed out of the room and into Anthony's bedroom, where the code letters and grille were still lying on the table. "Look, Freda," he said triumphantly to his wife, who had followed him into the room, "look – we've found him."

Can you read Anthony's message to his parents?

THE CASE OF THE FANCY FELINES

GLORIA GINSBERG, MILLIONAIRE NOVELIST AND CAT-LOVER, IS JUDGING THE **BEST IN SHOW** AT THE KENSINGTON CAT SHOW.

BORIS MOUSECOBITE

THAI-LONG

FEATHER FLUFFKINS

MINERS' TALE

SHE HAS TO CHOOSE BETWEEN CHAMPION **BORIS MOUSECOBITE**, THE RUSSIAN BLUE, CHAMPION **THAI-LONG**, THE SIAMESE, CHAMPION **FEATHER FLUFFKINS**, THE CHINCHILLA, AND CHAMPION **MINERS' TALE**, THE MANX.

AS SHE LEANS ACROSS THE TABLE HER DIAMOND-ENCRUSTED WATCH FALLS OFF HER WRIST...

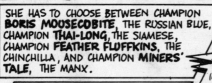

61

The Strange Case of the Prancing Pop Star

When Fiero Ricardo first headed the Top Twenty with his record "Gonna Dance All Night" his fans went wild. He was just nineteen, with the kind of dark, dashing good looks and proud Latin bearing that made the girls go weak. Even their mums, whose attention was caught by the slim athletic figure and flashing dark eyes, thought what an attractive lad he was, even though he leapt about on stage like a demented marionette.

His photograph appeared in endless pop magazines, to be torn out and stuck onto thousands of bedroom walls. Interviews appeared too, in which he told his fans all about his favourite records, films, TV programmes, food, pastimes and holiday places. He came, he said, from North London, of Spanish parentage, though both parents were now dead. What he didn't say, and what few knew, was that he was the son of the deposed president of Minarqua, a turbulent Latin American state. To his fans he was simply Fiero Ricardo, a fantastic singer and performer of fabulous songs.

His father, Alfonso Sarto, had not been heard of for the last eight months. Officially he was "in exile", but there were dark rumours that he had been murdered by the Fuego Rojo, the terrorist extremists who wanted to take over the country.

But Ricardo had managed to keep all this well hidden, and not even the most sensationalist press had ever hinted at it.

All through the spring months of that fateful year Ricardo's popularity increased. His fans grew even wilder, and every concert was followed by reports of mass hysteria, with girls fainting and having to be carried off in ambulances. Sales of his records rivalled those of Oasis and it seemed as if there was no peak he could not scale. But although his records sold worldwide, and his videos appeared on pop programmes on television from San Francisco to Singapore, he never travelled out of England. At first his agent, Bernie Goldsmith, put the lack of enthusiasm for foreign travel down to Ricardo's youth – after all, the lad had a lot on his plate for one so young. But as that amazingly successful spring turned into summer the pressure on Ricardo to travel became tremendous. His fans wanted to see him, they were tired of films and videos. Goldsmith told him plainly that, if he wanted to continue to be successful, he would have to do a concert tour. He put forward every argument he could think of, and Ricardo began to realize that he was right, and that he could refuse no longer.

And so a huge, open-air concert was arranged in the States for 11th August – a concert which would be watched by a live audience of 600,000 people, as well as the millions who would see the TV broadcast over various satellite links. And if that were not enough, the whole performance was to be filmed on video, to be sold to the fans who had missed it, or who just wanted the chance to see it again. And again. It was to be the pop music world's event of the year.

Fiero Ricardo put his foot down firmly against the idea of an American tour, though. "I'll go and do the concert, and that's all," he said. "Immediately afterwards I want to fly back to London."

Bernie Goldsmith, who was arranging a big party in his honour for the end of the concert, said nothing. The lad just had nerves, he decided. Once the concert was over, and a great success, as it was bound to be, he would relax a little. He might even be persuaded to go on tour – who knows!

The great day dawned. A sleek black Mercedes whisked Ricardo from his home in

St John's Wood in London to Heathrow Airport, to board his flight on Concorde. He had insisted on chartering the entire plane despite the cost. Bernie Goldsmith thought it was a waste of money, but put it down to the young singer's desire to impress his fans with his wealth.

Ricardo had refused to stay in an American hotel and had instead rented a private apartment in a quiet and unfashionable district on the outskirts of the city in which the concert was to be held. Goldsmith was surprised, but put it down to eccentricity, and the classic stars' ploy of pretending to escape from the public eye.

Pretence or not, it seemed to work. Apart from the tumultuous welcome at the airport and the near-mobbing of his white Cadillac as it swished away, he was left alone. His address had been kept a well-guarded secret.

He was not to be there long, however, for at eight o'clock that evening he strode on stage to a deafening roar of applause. Dressed in a shiny satin fuchsia pink shirt and tight-fitting silver-spangled white jeans, Ricardo was certainly an eye-catching figure. He sang his first number, "Spanish Rock", while gyrating round the stage to its pulsating rhythm, and the fans went wild. They quietened down a bit for the second, "Lookin' at You, Eyes of Blue", a moody love song. Then came the moment they'd all been waiting for. Ricardo swung into "Gonna Dance All Night" – swaying, leaping, spinning round, waving his arms and legs about in a frenzy of demented animation. Fans leapt into the air, screaming, jumped over seats and shouted until they were hoarse. The noise was deafening. Suddenly Ricardo did one of his famous stops – jerked in the air, stood still, wavered slightly, then, very slowly, began to wave his arms about as if he were in a hypnotic trance. The band had kept playing, though they wondered at the change in routine. Goldsmith looked concerned. "What's he doing? Is he ill?" But the sharper eyes in the audience could see a spreading red stain darken the fuchsia shirt and seep slowly down to the silver-white trousers. Ricardo sank to his knees, and keeled over.

It was some time before the audience realized what had happened. Figures rushed to and fro on the stage, but, after the briefest of pauses the band played on, albeit with a certain lack of enthusiasm. All except the lead guitar player, who had keeled over too and had to be carried out. He never could stand the sight of blood.

When all the rushing to and fro had stopped, so did the band. The master of ceremonies came on stage and addressed the audience. "I regret to announce that Fiero Ricardo and his lead guitarist have been taken ill. The concert will continue with Hank and the Heebie-Jeebies. Please stay in your seats until the performance is over."

But in a hospital casualty department a doctor was shaking his head at Bernie Goldsmith and saying, "I'm sorry, I'm afraid he's dead. He was shot in the stomach and died within minutes."

Lieutenant Ericsson of the police department was mystified. How could they find an assassin in a crowd of 600,000? And why should anyone want to kill this pop singer kid that the youngsters were all so keen on? Professional jealousy? Suddenly he remembered that the performance was being filmed on video. "Quick," he said to his men, "go and get the film off those guys. Let's see if it shows anything."

The film crew were only too happy to oblige, and an hour later they were assembled in a darkened room at police headquarters with a number of detectives, Lieutenant Ericsson and Bernie Goldsmith. They sat through the first two songs, all except Goldsmith wondering how anyone could stand the noise, then Ricardo got going on "Gonna Dance All Night". His frenzied dancing attracted attention. "Gee, how does that guy do it?" asked Ericsson. "He looks like he's got an electric charge running through him."

Suddenly Ricardo jerked and stopped. A small red mark appeared on the front of his shirt. He swayed on his feet, looked as if he were about to fall, then began a strange, slow, trance-like movements of his arms. It lasted a few moments while the red mark spread ever larger, then he sank to his knees and fell over.

"Can you slow the film down?" rapped out the Lieutenant.

"Sure," replied Ed, one of the camera boys.

"If what I'm thinking is right," said Ericsson, "this guy must have been in the rangers or in the navy. I think he's trying to signal to someone in semaphore."

Sure enough, when the film was slowed down, Ricardo's arm movements looked like those in the drawing opposite. On the following page you will find the semaphore alphabet.

Can you work out what Ricardo was trying to say?

THE CASE OF THE PERFECT PRINTS

FOUR CLEVER CAR THIEVES, ALL KNOWN TO THE POLICE, ARE WAITING FOR THE CHANCE TO STEAL LORD MIMSBURY'S BEAUTIFUL HISPANO-SUIZA.

THE CAR IS KEPT LOCKED IN ITS GARAGE, AND LORD MIMSBURY THINKS IT IS SAFE...

BUT— ONE MORNING...

A Death on the Ocean Wave

Hiram B Hockelheimer was not a popular man. He was rich, good-looking and very successful in business, but his ruthlessness had made him a number of enemies.

Hiram was in his forties, and his wife, the former Olympic athlete Emma Jane Robertson, was twelve years younger. They had been married for seven years when Hiram decided to take her on a Mediterranean cruise for her birthday present.

It was mid-September, and the calm golden days passed pleasantly. Hiram and Emma Jane sunbathed on deck, swam in the pool, dressed elegantly for dinner at the Captain's table, and dutifully visited the various sites of historical interest at which the ship called. It should have been an idyllic holiday, but Hiram was in reality itching to get back to his New York office. Also he was beginning to get irritated by the presence on the ship of his brother, Lester. He hadn't wanted Lester to come, but Lester had insisted. Hiram had felt in the last year or so that Lester was getting too fond of Emma Jane, though both of them denied it.

Hiram had also been upset by the discovery, on the second day out, that his arch-rival Grant Patterson was on board. It was well known in Wall Street circles that the two men disliked and mistrusted each other, and on the ship they kept well apart.

Emma Jane, however, was determined to try and enjoy her holiday, despite her husband's attitude. She had never been to Europe, and she was delighted to see places like Athens and Rome, which she found even more beautiful than she had imagined. Besides, over the years she had got used to ignoring her husband. She had got tired of his endless business deals and conferences and felt it was time she returned to her own life. She had recently taken up her athletics training again and intended to get a job tutoring schoolchildren who showed promise in track events. Hiram had agreed that when they returned to the States she could do that, and when she got tired of his tantrums she spent her time planning her new career.

On the Wednesday afternoon Emma Jane was reclining on a deck chair, reading a novel, when a shadow fell over her. It was Lester, who said urgently, "Emma, I've got to talk to you."

"What about?" Emma Jane did not sound encouraging.

"You don't love Hiram. Why don't you divorce him and marry me? You'd be much happier."

"No, I wouldn't, Lester. I don't love you, and I never will. I wish you'd leave me alone, once and for all."

Lester was about to protest when the approach of another figure stopped him. It was George Simpson, who had been Hiram's personal assistant for the past fifteen years.

"Excuse me, madam. Mr Hiram asked me to remind you that you and he are taking tea with the Venables at 4 pm."

Emma Jane sighed. "Yes, thank you George. I'll go and get dressed." She loathed these polite tea parties, which Hiram only arranged in order to further his business contacts. As she was getting ready she heard voices outside her cabin door. They were those of Lester and George Simpson. The latter was speaking.

"Mr Lester, I have no liking for your brother either, but I cannot do as you ask. It is out of the question. I am waiting until I have saved enough money from my salary to start my own small business, and then I shall leave Mr Hiram for good."

She wondered what they were talking about, as she had had no suspicion that Simpson even thought of leaving her husband's employment.

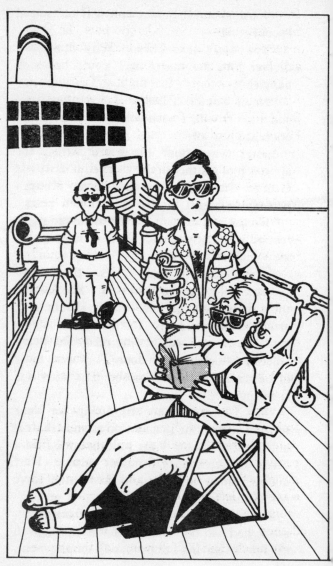

It was reassuring that he disliked Hiram too. She had always wondered how he had managed to put up with the barked commands and bad temper for so long.

The ship anchored that night at Taormina in Sicily and some of the passengers went ashore for dinner. Among them was Grant Patterson, Hiram noticed with relief. He, Lester and Emma Jane remained on board with the McCarter party, as Hiram wanted to discuss the outlook for certain kinds of shares with old Mr McCarter, who had the reputation of being something of a financial wizard. His wife was addressing Emma Jane. "So you hope to resume your career soon, my dear? It sounds very exciting."

"Yes, I'm looking forward to it very much," replied Emma Jane. "In fact. . ."

She was interrupted by her husband. "I've been thinking, honey, that it might not be such a good idea after all. I don't think my employees will think too highly of a boss who lets his wife work."

Emma Jane was about to protest when the look in his eye stopped her. He might have sounded friendly enough, but that was just because they were with other people. He meant what he said all right. As soon as she could she left the party and returned to her cabin, feeling wretched now all her hopes were dashed.

At lunch time the following day the ship set

sail for North Africa. By the evening a storm was blowing up, the wind whipping up the sea into foam, and dark clouds spoiling the September sunshine. The passengers ate their dinner uneasily – the more faint-hearted had already retired to their cabins.

"I see Patterson's back," growled Hiram. "I'd hoped he'd stay in Taormina."

"I bet he wishes he had now," said Emma as Patterson, his face a ghastly colour, hastily excused himself and left the salon. She was not feeling too well herself, though Hiram and Lester seemed quite unaffected by the roughness of the sea.

After the meal Lester went to play cards with Bill and Louise Henderson. Emma Jane said she would go to bed early, but Hiram decided to take a walk round the deck as he found the storm invigorating. It was 9.30 pm.

Mrs Evan Williams later testified that she heard signs of a struggle, followed by a heavy splash, at about ten o'clock. She had rushed out of her cabin to see a figure bobbing in the water – a figure that kept disappearing under the waves. She raised the alarm and a boat was lowered into the heaving sea and, at great risk to themselves, the sailors succeeded in heaving the figure out of the water. But by this time it was a corpse – the corpse of Hiram B Hockelheimer.

Who pushed him overboard?

A Message from the Dead

The scene was the common room of Eldonbridge University, known throughout the world for the prowess of its archaeology professors and their students. The university had a museum, whose collection rivalled that of the British Museum in London – in fact some said it was a great deal better, for it was quality not quantity that counted. The staff were currently involved in arranging an exhibition of ancient Chinese artefacts, found by Professors Wentworth and Faulkner while excavating a tomb near Samarkand, just off the ancient silk route. Professor Wentworth had been a highly respected member of staff at Eldonbridge; Professor Faulkner had come originally from an American university, and had been working with him on his studies.

The excavations had taken place more than ten years earlier. Why had the exhibition taken so long to organize? Young Bob Brown, a first-year student, addressed the question to Professor Townsend, who was taking a short break from his task of overseeing the setting up of the exhibits.

"Ah, well, Brown, you see the treasure was found – and then lost again."

"Sounds very careless," said Bob. "It was Professors Wentworth and Faulkner who found it, wasn't it? In 1974?"

"That's right," replied the professor.

"So how did they lose the treasure? And what happened to them? They no longer work here, do they?"

"The answer to those questions is rather a long story," smiled Townsend. "If you really want to hear about it, come to my study and I'll tell you. We don't say too much about it in public at Eldonbridge."

When they were seated in the study, and Professor Townsend had selected a file from the shelves and placed it on his desk, he continued.

"Brian Wentworth and Gerald Faulkner set off on the expedition on 1st February 1974. They spent several months carefully searching the area in which they believed the tomb to be, and, on 26th May, sent a letter to the university saying: 'We believe we are almost there. We have found an ante-chamber with carved statues wearing jade collars, and we believe that it is only a matter of time before we find the inner chamber. The indications are that the treasures within will surpass belief.'

"That was the last we heard from them. Colleagues tried to make contact without success, and when officials from the Soviet government were approached all they would say was that the men had packed their belongings and gone. They didn't know whether any treasure had been found, but the caves referred to in Wentworth's letter were empty. One report indicated that when the two men had gone away one of them was tied up and appeared to be struggling, but no one knew if this was true, nor, if it were, which one of the men was tied up. It looked very much like a conspiracy between Wentworth and Faulkner to steal the treasure.

"We, at Eldonbridge, were very anxious to clear the professors' names, especially that of our old and trusted colleague Brian Wentworth. We managed to keep the matter out of the papers, and sent a party of men to the USSR to investigate. At first it seemed as if they had found nothing. Two caves had been excavated, but they contained nothing except a few human bones. There were hieroglyphics and the remains of paintings on the cave walls, but no one could find any clue as to what had happened until one of the archaeologists, who had been studying the hieroglyphics, exclaimed, 'Hello! This isn't ancient Chinese writing! We may have found a clue at last.'

"There, amongst the half-faded plants, animals and people depicted in the frieze, and annotated with Chinese characters, was this."

Professor Townsend opened the file on his desk and took out a large photograph. He handed it to Bob who saw:

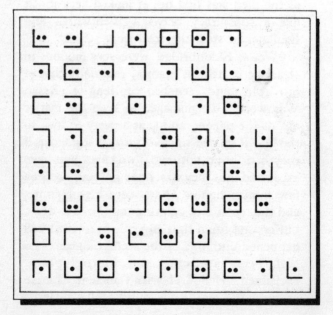

"Well, it cleared Wentworth's name, though it didn't help us find him or get the treasure back. Then one day, years later, a herdsman searching for his strayed sheep stumbled across another cave. Inside he found a human skeleton - and packing cases full of treasure. The skeleton proved to be that of Faulkner. His diary read: 'I can't go on, the fever is so bad. Perhaps it's God's vengeance for what I did to Brian. But he was such a fool, wanting to take the treasure back to Eldonbridge!'

"So you see," said Professor Townsend, "it seems that Faulkner killed Wentworth and stole the treasure for himself, though how he hoped to dispose of it no one knows. But we at Eldonbridge were glad Wentworth's name was cleared, even though it was at the expense of his colleague's."

"I can see that the diary entry cleared Wentworth," said Bob, "but how did that peculiar message in the cave? I suppose it was a message?"

"It's a well-known cipher called the Rosicrucian cipher," replied Townsend. "Wentworth was rather fond of puzzles and ciphers. Here is one of his notebooks. It will help you to work out the message."

Overleaf is what Bob read.

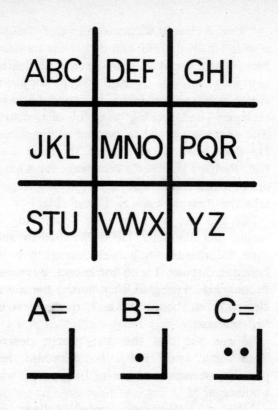

With its help, can you decipher Professor Wentworth's message?

Midnight Meeting

The thin November rain fell steadily that night, covering the Whitechapel pavements with a greasy film which reflected the moon's beams. Nothing stirred in the dingy streets except a small, thin tabby cat, which picked its way daintily round the puddles. Its curiosity had been aroused by a large, dark object, lying motionless in the gutter. . .

That same object was discovered by an early morning shift worker, just as light was returning to the grim streets. He rushed back to his house and phoned the police.

By lunch time the news had become public, for the body had been identified. It was that of Luigi Minelli, wanted by police in seven countries for murder, smuggling, and suspected terrorist activities.

The police machinery began to move into action. In charge of the case was Detective

Superintendent Crawford, a brilliant young policeman, who had risen to his exalted position very quickly. He was assisted by Detective Sergeant Wilkins and Detective Constable Rouse. It was the morning after Minelli's body had been found, and Crawford was running over the facts of the case.

"From the post mortem we know that Minelli was shot in the back, probably about midnight on the 14th, and we think his body was dumped in Smeaton Street, Whitechapel, some time later. There was very little blood where the body was found, indicating that the shooting had taken place elsewhere.

"Reg Copley reported finding the body at 6.40 am. It can't have been there long, or surely someone else would have found it."

"It could be they did, sir." Constable Rouse was more familiar with the back streets of Whitechapel than was his superior. "A lot of people who live round those parts would go home and bolt the door if they found a body in the street in the middle of the night. They know better than to interfere with the likes of Minelli."

The names of Minelli and the other members of the gang with which he operated had become synonymous with terror in that part of Whitechapel. Their London headquarters was there, and they were known and recognized by the local people, but had an uncanny knack of disappearing when the police arrived on the scene. Minelli wouldn't disappear this time, though.

Crawford continued. "The most likely suspects are the other members of the gang. They all hated him and had reasons for wanting him dead. Those believed to be in London on the night of the 14th/15th are Jimmy McPherson, the Glasgow knife-man, Charlie Evans, chief suspect in the embassy poisoning case, and François Duval, implicated in the Marseilles smuggling ring. They are all known to have handled guns at some time or another. I want each man checked out – their particular motives, their movements that night, their alibis, if any. Note down anything you discover about them – it may help us prove that they committed the earlier crimes of which we suspect them, but which we've not been able to pin on them for lack of evidence."

"What about Tina Torova, sir? She and Minelli might have had a lovers' quarrel."

"Yes," replied Crawford. "I'd thought of that. *I'm* going to see Miss Torova at that club where she works – the *White Pelican*, isn't it?"

Wilkins nodded and sighed. Trust the chief to suss out the blonde while he and Rouse had to pound the seamy streets of Whitechapel looking for far less attractive customers.

They found Charlie Evans having an early lunch-time drink at the *Pig and Whistle*. When he saw Wilkins walk in, he tried to get out through the back door but was met by Rouse, who led him back to the bar.

"Just want a friendly chat, Charlie. About where you've been for the last couple of days – and, in particular, where you were on the night of the 14th."

"Night of the 14th, guv? I was at home, watching the telly. It was the night the big fight was on, so I got myself a few bottles of beer in and put my feet up in front of the telly. Nice to have a quiet night occasionally."

"Who was with you, Charlie?" asked Wilkins casually.

"With me? No one – I like a bit of time to myself."

"And you live just round the corner from Smeaton Street, don't you Charlie?"

"I live at 19 Wharf Lane, as you well know," retorted Charlie. "It's near Smeaton Street. What of it?"

"What have you done to your hand, Charlie?" asked Rouse, eyeing the disreputable-looking plaster on Charlie's right forearm. "Fall downstairs?"

"That's right," said Charlie nastily. "You lot ought to know – some of your mob were there at that fiasco last week."

Rouse and Wilkins prepared to leave. "Buy yourself a drink, Charlie," said the latter, tossing over a £1 coin. Charlie made a grab with his left hand before it fell to the floor.

François Duval was a very different kind of criminal. Tall, dark, sleek, expensively dressed, he was playing roulette in a West End gambling club when the two detectives found him. He was coldly polite, and not at all helpful. On the night of the 14th he had been at the same club, he said. Witnesses remembered seeing him having dinner about nine, and later playing poker, though they were not quite sure of the time. But the manager confirmed he had been there at 1.15 am, for he had won rather a lot of money and the croupier had called the manager to make sure all was well with the bet.

As they left, Wilkins turned round to look at Duval. He appeared to be fingering a small, rigid object in the right-hand pocket of his dinner jacket.

Jimmy McPherson, nicknamed Mac the Knife, was the kind of man who made Rouse and Wilkins glad they were together. Over six foot tall, stockily built and with a wild look about him, he was suspected of having knifed several people, though nothing had ever been proved. But of all the suspects, Jimmy seemed to be the one with the cast-iron alibi. He had been seen boarding the Glasgow train at 11pm that night – a train that didn't stop until Leicester – which ruled out the possibility of having killed Minelli at midnight.

Rouse and Wilkins returned to Scotland Yard.

Meanwhile their boss had been interviewing Minelli's girlfriend, Tina Torova. A well-built glamorous blonde, she sang sultry songs at the *White Pelican Club*, just around the corner from Smeaton Street. But today she looked tired and drab. She looked, thought Crawford, as if she'd been crying – if that were possible.

She didn't like policemen and was less than polite to Crawford. Eventually he got out of her that she had been on stage at ten and eleven, but had missed her later appearances as she had felt tired and had gone to bed early. No one could prove that was true.

"We know you have a gun licence," said Crawford. "May I see your gun?"

After some protest she produced a small pearl-handled pistol.

"I must tell you that we believe it was a gun of this type that killed Minelli," said Crawford.

"Well, it wasn't mine," spat out Torova. "I loved Luigi – and I'd no reason to kill him. He was much more use to me alive than dead."

And Crawford was inclined to believe her.
Who killed Luigi Minelli?

94

... AND THE ONLY OTHER PEOPLE WHO COULD POSSIBLY HAVE ENTERED HER ROOM ARE:

HER DRESSMAKER, TWEASEL TWEND, WHO OWNS A STRING OF BOUTIQUES —

HER HAIRDRESSER, LANGUID LOCKS, WHO DOES THE HAIR OF MANY OF THE RICH AND FAMOUS —

AND HER AUNT AUGUSTA, WHO RUNS AN ANTIQUES BUSINESS IN HER SPARE TIME.

WHODUNNIT?

A Day at the Circus

It was the week before Christmas and Chesterman's Circus was in full swing. The Big Top was full of excited children who oohed and aahed at the daring exploits of the tightrope walkers and trapeze artistes, marvelled at the well-trained elegance of the liberty horses, and laughed till their sides ached at the antics of the clowns. There was absolutely no sign that all was not well behind the scenes.

The sad truth was that it was the last few days of Charlie Chesterman's management of the circus. For fifty years he had been in charge, running the show from his caravan, and now all was to change. Charlie had an incurable disease, and though his mind was still agile his body was not. In recent months he had had to succumb to life in a wheelchair. The onset of winter had made everyone in the family realize that he could no longer continue to live in the caravan and oversee the day to day running of the circus, so he had agreed to go and live in a comfortable home for the disabled and visit the circus as often as he could. The general management of the show, and, on his death, the ownership of it, was to pass to his teenage daughter, Charmian, who thrilled the crowds with her prowess on the tightrope. Charmian was disappointed that she would have less time to spend practising her tightrope routines, but pleased at the thought of running the circus. She was an ambitious girl, and though she was the apple of her father's eye, and "a true Chesterman", she could see how certain changes would benefit the circus and she intended carrying them out.

However, old Charlie's decision was not popular with the rest of the family. Charmian's mother had died when her daughter was still a child, and in due course Charlie had married Annie Shepherd, known to circus fans as Madame Anita, who performed with a troupe of trained poodles. Annie Shepherd had been married to George Shepherd, the circus's former ringmaster, but he had run off with an acrobat and left Annie to bring up her son, Ian, alone. Ian was now seventeen, two years younger than Charmian, but both he and his mother felt that running a circus was a man's job, and Annie had tried to persuade old Charlie to leave the circus to Ian. But Charlie was adamant. Charmian might be a girl but he could see that she had all the right qualities to run the

circus. She was a clever girl, with lots of commonsense. She had the makings of a tough businesswoman, but she treated the staff fairly and was concerned with the welfare of the animals. The liberty horses had a holiday each year when the circus took a month off at its summer quarters on a farm in Shropshire, the dogs were regularly exercised and well fed, and Charmian personally saw that Katy, the one elephant, did not perform silly and undignified tricks that made her uncomfortable, but rather carried out tasks which demonstrated her strength, agility and obedience, as a working elephant should. Ian, on the other hand, was an ambitious young man with a ruthless streak, who had been known to treat both staff and animals unkindly. His attitude was that, as the boss's stepson, everyone and everything should do as he wished and as he said. Old Charlie did not like this attitude and saw that it foretold a troubled future for the circus, so he took no notice of his wife's pleading of her son's case. This, of course, did not please Annie, and slowly her attitude towards her husband hardened. She began to find him irritating, and his disabilities annoyed her. The Chesterman family was not a very happy one.

But the unhappiness only strengthened Charmian's love for her father and her determination to carry out his wishes. And, for the forthcoming Boxing Day show, the last performance with Charlie actively running the circus, she had worked out a specially daring routine which involved dancing on the tightrope and was performed without a safety net. It was to be a surprise for Charlie – a sort of farewell present. She hoped the excitement wouldn't be too much for him, for his heart was not very strong, but she had consulted his doctor who had said that provided everything went according to plan his heart should suffer no ill effects.

Her final practice was on Boxing Day morning, before the afternoon's performance. The current ringmaster, Jim Biggins, who didn't care much for Charmian and sided with Ian and Annie in thinking they needed a man to run the circus, watched her. He had to admit she was very good – all the more reason, he thought, for her to stick to tightrope walking and not get involved in running the circus. When she was back on the ground again he congratulated her.

"Thanks, Jim," said Charmian. "I think I've got it about right. I just need to adjust the fixing on the right-hand end of the rope slightly, to give it a bit more bounce."

"I'll see to it," said Jim, for it was really his job to make sure all the props were in order. "You go and have something to eat. You've got to keep your strength up, you know."

After lunch, the ringmaster went into the Big Top again to check that all was ready for the performance. The tent was empty except for Ian, who was walking across the ring. "Hello, Ian," said the ringmaster. "Having a last minute practice?"

"That's right," replied Ian. His voice was sarcastic. "Everything's got to be perfect this afternoon, hasn't it?"

"You bet," said Jim. "We'll give old Charlie a performance to remember."

Ian went out of the ring to get into his costume for his trapeze act. Jim was still checking things when Annie Chesterman came in to say he was wanted on the phone. He went out of the Big Top leaving Annie in the ring, gazing up at the tightrope.

By four o'clock the audience was sitting with baited breath waiting for the beginning of the show. Charlie Chesterman had the seat of honour, and his wife and daughter sat with him, in their costumes, until it was time for their acts. There was a roll on the drums, a fanfare of trumpets, and in came Jim, resplendent in his red coat and shiny black top hat to introduce the first act, a group of acrobats from Japan. They were slick and clever and got a good round of applause, which changed to hearty laughter when, towards the end of the act, the clowns came tumbling in to create chaos. The audience loved it.

Then it was time for the liberty horses. They were all pure-bred Arabians, grey in colour, some darkly dappled and some almost white, and they trotted daintily into the ring, their necks arched and tails held out like banners. In perfect unison they wheeled, pirouetted, changed their paces from a trot to a canter and back again, walked on their hind legs, and bowed gracefully to the audience at the end.

Madame Anita was on next with her merry little dogs, whose bouncy cheerfulness contrasted well with the elegance of the horses. Charlie thought he'd never seen a better performance and applauded loudly. Annie's act was followed by a brief appearance by the clowns, and she was back at Charlie's side by the time Charmian's act was announced. Of Ian, who was to follow Charmian, there was no sign.

Charmian, in her short-skirted silver-sequinned dress and tights, ran daintily to the foot of the ladder and began to climb to where the rope was stretched high above the sawdust ring. When she reached the top she turned to smile and wave to the audience – and Charlie knew it was a special smile for him. The audience held its breath as she walked across the wire, and clapped loudly when she reached the far side. She began to return, and when she reached the very centre of the rope, did a few dance steps to test its springiness. Those blessed with good eyesight might have noticed a slightly puzzled look cross her face, and she paused for a moment before continuing her special dance routine. But as she bounced on the rope it was obvious to those with trained eyes that something was wrong. The rope was too loose. She wavered for a moment, tried to regain her balance, and suddenly fell. The ringmaster, and two clowns who had been watching from the side of the ring, ran in and managed to break her fall. The four of them crumpled to the ground in a heap in the centre of the ring. People in the audience were screaming. A St John's Ambulance man rushed towards the bodies while his colleague ran to get the ambulance. In his wheelchair old Charlie Chesterman had gone as white as a sheet, and his head slumped forwards on his chest.

But Charlie was not dead. He had fainted, and he soon came round, though he was very badly shaken. Annie was shaken too, and wondered what on earth could have gone wrong. Charmian was usually so careful.

Meanwhile Charmian was on her way to hospital, unconscious and with multiple fractures.

Who tampered with the rope?

ANSWERS

The Case of the Valuable Valentines

The customer on the left of the picture at the bottom of page 6, with the cigarette in a holder. He has dropped the butt on the floor by the case.

The Case of the Extraordinary Easter Eggs

The message reads: CARLOS STRUCK. TELL MI 5. JACK.

Mrs Pearson did contact MI 5 who, after swearing her to secrecy, explained that Carlos was an internationally wanted criminal, suspected of espionage and terrorist activities, and that her husband had had to go off on his trail. They could not say when he would be back — though he did eventually return six months later. It all took a lot of explaining in the village without giving the game away, but the Pearsons managed it and their life returned to the same pattern as before. Jack Pearson gave up eating eggs, and there were no more special treats at Easter. But he made fewer visits to his mother, and when he did go, he stayed away for a shorter time.

By the way, this method of writing on eggs uses alum, a white powder, mixed with vinegar, and the message is written on the egg's shell, where it remains invisible. It is only when the egg is boiled that the message reveals itself on the egg white. The method was used in the First

World War to carry secret messages behind enemy lines. It is not advisable to try it yourself. The alum powder would sting if it got on your skin, and the mixture would make you ill if you ate it!

A Likely Winner

Dave Duncan. He hated Bridges and wanted to win the Newmarket Cup very much – and knew he had no chance with Bridges and Set Fair in the race. He knew a lot about cars and could have cut the pipe when the car was parked outside Bridges' house the night before. Neither Charlie Taylor nor Terry Griggs knew enough about cars to have cut the brake pipe.

The Case of the Driffield Diamond

The lady with the bun stole the diamond – she left a hairpin lying on the floor by the case.

The Fanshawe Family Mystery

The message read: *Have important evidence first Rupert is not your nephew. Take this letter to Scotland Yard at once.* The letter used what is called a pin-hole code, in which small holes are made under words in an innocent-looking document. When the document is held up to the light, the holes are revealed, and the message can be read, the words with holes under them making up the message. In this book the holes have been replaced with small black dots.

You can use a pinhole code to send secret messages to your friends.

A Shot in the Dark

Jennifer Latham killed Lily Lajeune. Only three people had strong enough motives – Henry Proctor, Jennifer and Selma Price. Both Henry and Selma were in their dressing-rooms at that part of the play, but Jennifer left the stage before the rest of the cast and had time to get herself into position to fire the shot.

The Case of the Missing Manuscript

The only person who could have stolen the manuscript is the man with the umbrella, as he is the only one with a place to hide it.

Shopping for Gold

The shopping list is a code, the number of pence beside each item indicating which letter of it the reader should note. So "fish fingers 1p/5p" means "F", "ice-cream 1p" means "I" and so on.

The typing agency turned out to be run by a well-known internationally wanted criminal, the agency simply being a front for his activities. He used the girls to find out what was going on in the firms at which they worked, and to turn the information into a shopping list code. This they would pass to a contact whom they would "accidentally" bump into in the street at a pre-arranged time on certain days. The contact in turn passed on the information to the boss, who organized a gang to carry out the robberies.

Take a Bow

Maria Oliver killed Grandfather. She knew a lot more about her children's desperation than they realized, and, unknown to them, had always disliked her husband's father. She had been good at archery in her youth, and simply picked up Fenton's spare bow and hid behind the trees bordering the drive to make her shot.

The Case of the Sinister Safe

The man painting the window frame on the left of the picture at the bottom of page 51 is the only person who could have opened the safe apart from Colonel Smythson-Smythe.

The Greek Island Kidnap

The message reads: '*In ammonia* square third on right come soon.*' *Ammonia is a way of using an ordinary word to mean a name. In Athens there is place called Omonia Square, and Anthony knew that his parents would recognize the name. He could not write it out properly or the kidnappers would have been suspicious.

Mr Llewellyn read the message by putting the code grille over Anthony's letter, as his son had hoped he would. Compare the letter with code grille on page 55.

The Case of the Fancy Felines

The owner of Feather Fluffkins, the chinchilla, took it and hid it in his cat's fur.

The Strange Case of the Prancing Pop Star

Fiero Ricardo's message read: FUEGO ROJO GOT ME TOO. The terrorists who had shot his father had also shot him.

The Case of the Perfect Prints

Hotrod Horace. The tip of the index finger on his left hand is missing, as is that on the fingerprints.

A Death on the Ocean Wave

Emma Jane did. Lester was playing cards with the Hendersons, Grant Patterson was too ill, and George Simpson had said he would stay with Hockelheimer until he'd saved enough money to start on his own. Emma Jane couldn't bear the thought of a future as Hiram's wife with no life of her own, and her athletics training gave her sufficient strength to push him overboard.

The Case of the Groggy Greyhound

Inspector Hawkins is pointing to the man at the right-hand side of the bar, with fair hair and a dark jacket, as his footprints match those outside Whip-It-Quick's kennel.

A Message from the Dead

The message read: *I cannot trust F. He plans to steal the treasure. I fear for my life. Wentworth.*

Midnight Meeting

Françoise Duval killed Luigi Minelli. Charlie Evans had his right arm in plaster – and was right-handed, as shown by his failure to catch the coin Wilkins threw to him. Jimmy McPherson was not in London to do it and Tina Torova had no motive, even though she had the right kind of gun. But Duval had a similar gun which he fingered in his pocket as Rouse and Wilkins left.

The Case of the Plastic Pearls

The dressmaker, Tweasel Twend, took the necklace. It is wrapped round his left wrist. The other two suspects' necklaces are too short to be the stolen one.

A Day at the Circus

Ian tampered with the rope. He thought that with Charmian out of the way he would gain control of the circus, and he thought that the shock of her death would probably kill old Charlie, too. But he miscalculated the amount to slacken the rope, giving time for those below to see what was going to happen and to break Charmian's fall. She survived, and returned to the circus after a long stay in hospital, though there was no more tightrope walking for her. Ian disappeared and was never seen again.